Catty Jane
Who Hated the Rain

Written and Illustrated by
VALERI GORBACHEV

BOYDS MILLS PRESS
Honesdale, Pennyslvania

Boyds Mills Press, Inc.
815 Church Street
Honesdale, Pennsylvania 18431
Printed in China

ISBN: 978-1-59078-700-7

Library of Congress Control Number: 2011940117

First edition
The text of this book is set in 14-point Caxton Light.
The illustrations are done in watercolor and pen and ink.
10 9 8 7 6 5 4 3 2 1

For all my *Highlights* friends
—VG

Catty Jane did not like rainy days.
They were gray. And dreary. And wet.

"Why don't we read a book until the rain stops?" said Mama. "Or we could play a game. Would you like a cookie? I just baked some."

"No, thank you," said Catty Jane. "I don't want any cookies. I don't want to read or play a game. It's no use trying to cheer me up. I can't do *anything* when it's raining!"

"What a shame," said Mama. "Oh, look!
Your friends are here. Maybe Piggy and Froggy
and Goose can help you feel better."

"Hello, Mrs. Cat. Hi, Catty Jane. Isn't this a wonderful rainstorm?"
"Wonderful?" said Catty Jane. "It's terrible! I hate the rain!"
"Please come in, kids," said Mama.

"I love the rain," said Piggy. "I love taking a walk under my big, beautiful umbrella. I love wearing my pretty raincoat and matching boots."

"Not me," said Catty Jane. "I can't stand getting wet!"

"I love to stroll on the bridge and watch the raindrops splash into the river," said Froggy. "They make such a beautiful picture on the water."

"Not me," said Catty Jane. "I don't like being outside when it rains."

"I love to dance and sing in the rain," said Goose. "I'm not even afraid of thunder and lightning!"

"I'm afraid of thunder and lightning even when I'm inside," said Catty Jane.

"Who would like some cookies?" asked Mama.

"Yum! Thanks!" said Piggy. "Hey, I have a great idea! Let's have a rainy-day party right here in the house! Then Catty Jane won't have to worry about getting wet."

"A rainy-day party?" said Catty Jane. "What's that?"

"It's a party with cookies and umbrellas and dancing. It will be fun."

"I don't know if I would like that," said Catty Jane.

"I know a game we can play at our party," said Froggy. "We can pretend to be raindrops splashing into the Raindrops River."

"But what about the thunder and lightning?" asked Catty Jane.

"No problem!" said Goose. "Froggy and I will play music and you can dance. We'll make so much noise you won't hear the thunder."

"We can close the curtains so you won't see the lightning," said Piggy.

"Well, I do like to dance," said Catty Jane.

Soon they were having so much fun that Catty Jane forgot all about the rain.

"Look, the rain has stopped!" cried Froggy. "Now we can play outside."
"Hooray!" shouted the others. "Let's go!"

"Let's splash through the puddles!" cried Piggy. "Wheee!"

"Oh no!" said Catty Jane. "I don't like getting wet!"

"But I do love a rainy-day party!"